aidan chambers

Blindside

Barrington Stoke

First published in 2015 in Great Britain by
Barrington Stoke Ltd
18 Walker Street, Edinburgh, EH3 7LP

www.barringtonstoke.co.uk

This story was first published in a different form
as *Cycle Smash* (William Heinemann, 1967)

A CIP catalogue record for this book is available
from the British Library upon request

ISBN: 978-1-78112-464-2

Printed in China by Leo

Contents

1. The Harriers

The hot water struck Nate's body and he tensed and whistled with the pain. He added a touch of cold to make the shower cooler. As he stood there, with the water drumming on his skull, he smiled at the memory of the run. He liked to win, even if it was only a training run. He had been at least 100 metres in front of Jed.

Now Nate could hear Jed struggling out of his running gear in the changing room. Nate broke into a rowdy song that bounced off the tiles of the shower room. He thought again of the day when he would run against better men than this club ever took on.

Jed pranced in, with his hands clasped and his knuckles white. He was shivering from the cold. His skin was covered in goose-bumps and mud was caked on his legs. He tested the water with his foot.

"God! You've got it hot!" he said. "Put some more cold on."

Nate laughed. There was always a pantomime about the hot water.

Jed dithered. "Come on, mate. Some cold!" he said again.

Nate flicked water with the flat of his hand and Jed yelled.

"Get in and stop mucking about," Nate shouted.

Jed sprang in like a swimmer into the deep end. Nate laughed at his moans.

Out in the changing room, panting voices discussed the run. The others were coming in. Their bare feet flapped on the wooden floor.

"Freezing cold out there today," Jed said. His skin was turning red. Hot water spouted off the end of his nose.

"But good," Nate said. He rubbed himself with the flat of his hands. A shower always relaxed him, made him feel good. Jed looked at him as the water flattened his blond hair and streamed down his long limbs. Both their bodies steamed.

"You're too good a runner for this club," Jed said.

Nate shook his head. He never knew what to say when people praised him. "I know!" he said, and laughed.

Charlie splashed into the shower next to Nate. "Has it been a year already since your last bath?" he said.

Always the same jokes. Always from the same people. It was one of the things Nate liked about the club.

*****

Later on the changing room was crowded with hot bodies. The air was sour with sweat and people's socks were stinking.

Nate towelled himself dry as fast as he could and dressed. He combed his hair. It wasn't dry yet. Water dripped onto his neck and collar.

Ivor the club captain came in.

"I'll tell you what, Nate," he said in his Welsh accent, "you keep goin' in this form, boyo, and they'll snap you up for the National Cross Country this year."

Nate packed his bag to avoid answering. There was no need for the captain to tell him. He knew. But Nate was glad he had said it. It made it seem more likely to happen, not just a private dream of Nate's own.

"You'll have to keep off the girls then," Charlie said.

"It's the fried chicken you need to keep off, Charlie," Nate said. "You've got a right gut on you already."

He slapped Charlie's stomach hard. Charlie gulped and doubled up. The others laughed.

"You're getting lanky, Nate," Taylor said. He was another of the lads – a good runner, but not as good as Nate. "Too tall," Taylor went on. "You want some body on you. A bit of fried chicken wouldn't do you no harm – you'd feel stronger for it."

"Don't you go corrupting him," Ivor said. "Nate's OK. He's in fine fettle."

Taylor laughed. "He's a skinny kid, not a racehorse," he said.

Nate had had enough. He slung his bag on his back and slipped past Jed.

"See you, Ivor," he said. "So long everyone."

They all yelled back.

"See you Thursday," the captain shouted.

Nate waved and closed the changing-room door behind him.

2. A Game

Outside, the frost bit sharp on Nate's face and hands. There was soft mud where feet had churned up the ground. But as he walked away from the building, the grass was crisp and the frost crunched under his shoes. He took a deep breath and ran a few steps just to feel his legs do it again. It was like the memory of a moment of pleasure, and it was good. Very good. He hurled his bag high in the air and caught it, running forward and stooping, rugby-style.

Nate turned out of the field into the park and walked towards the road. Some kids were playing football. It was a noisy game with everyone on any and both sides, and coats for goal-posts. Nate joined in and stopped a loose ball with the inside of his foot. Boys rushed to him. He took off and chased across the white frosty field, his breath hanging misty behind him.

To the boys, his easy pace looked nothing at first. But when the biting air dug at their lungs, they saw how fast he was and some stopped chasing. Nate shot the ball into goal.

"You can't half run," a boy called.

"Let's get on," someone yelled.

"You shouldn't have let that in, Ben," another boy shouted at the goalie. "Come on!"

"It doesn't count anyway," the goalie shouted, as he kicked the ball away. "He's not even playing."

Nate waved.

From the park gates, the boys looked all feet and thin black shapes. Nate remembered days like that – games that ended in fights at dark, when the two or three park lights came on, yellow pools that deepened the evening into night.

"Nate!"

He looked back. Jed was bellowing at him across the field. He stopped. Jed broke into a run, his kit flapping in his hands. He never remembered to bring a bag.

They walked together to the main road. Houses reached away on the other side from the park – semi-detached with bay windows, roses in the gardens, wood fences and pavements with trees between the lamp-posts.

Cars and lorries and buses rumbled past.

"Going out tonight?" Jed asked.

"Maybe," Nate said. "Why?"

"Listen," Jed said, "I saw this girl at the pool hall the other night. God, Nate! She was fit."

Nate grinned. "Fine. You'll enjoy yourself."

Jed put a hand on Nate's arm. "Look, mate. How long have we known each other? Since the days when we were like those kids in the park? And how old are we now? You need to get out more. Life's not just about running and school work."

"You know what it is, Jed?" Nate said with a smile. "I run better than you do. I ride a bike better than you ..."

"So ...?"

"So I don't want to get into your games with girls," Nate said. His face was grave now. "I might beat you at that too. Then what would you do? You'd have nothing to boast about."

Jed punched him. "You know what I like about you? Your shining modesty. Your low opinion of yourself. You're so humble! But how about it, Nate? The pool hall tonight?"

"Maybe," Nate said. "I don't know."

"I need the back-up, mate," Jed pleaded.

"OK," Nate said. "When?"

"7.30."

"I'll be there."

3. Pedals

They walked together down to Jed's. Jed lived at the bottom of the road in a bungalow, with his mum. His dad had died of a brain tumour when he was a little boy and now his mum spent half her time worrying about Jed. But she was OK. At least she didn't nag.

"Clear off," Jed said when they reached his gate.

"See you," Nate said.

Nate had left his bike on Jed's drive. He unlocked it, wheeled it onto the road and got on.

Nate pushed down hard on the pedals and sped off down the road. He loved being on a bike and he was saving all he could to buy a top-of-the-range pro model, meant for fast and agile riding. It would have to be second hand. A new one would cost far too much. He might be able to get it cheap if it needed work to get it into good shape again. But he would like it all the more for that.

Next to a good run, his bike was the thing Nate loved most. But running was a serious business. He dreamed of the day when he might compete against those incredible runners from Kenya and Ethiopia. And it wasn't just a dream. Ivor believed he could do it. So did loads of the other lads in the club. Even Jed did, for all he wouldn't say so.

But bikes were something Nate could enjoy messing about with. He liked that sense of speed and skill, but without the stress and strain of a race. A bike was for fun.

The pedals hummed in their smooth circles. The sound echoed from the houses as Nate passed. And then the noise was swallowed in the blaze of town traffic on the main road.

There was a narrow, 90-degree turn, where the road ran down into the town centre. Nate slowed right down to cross into the road that led to his house. He wondered again why there weren't traffic lights there. You couldn't see anything coming at you up the hill. And a lot of drivers put their foot down to clear the corner. One day someone would get killed.

4. Ink

At 7.30 that night, on his way to meet Jed, it was Nate who was nearly killed.

When he got home he'd changed and had supper. The run had left him hungry. His parents were used to his appetite, but even they looked amazed as Nate wolfed down two jacket potatoes and three helpings of salad.

"Better to keep a week than a fortnight," his mother said.

"Them long legs," his father said. "Hollow, they are."

Nate's father was a quiet man who liked reading and cooking and listening to music. He often wondered how it could be that his son was such a runner.

Nate put on his jacket and his bike helmet. It wasn't far to the pool hall, and he couldn't be bothered to change again when he got there.

Outside, the night air was chisel-sharp against Nate's face. The speed of the bike cutting through the cold air made the first few metres painful. His front light sparkled on crystal pin-pricks of frost on the road. He was careful not to make sudden movements.

At the junction onto the main road, he came to a careful stop.

Shops blocked the view down the hill. Nate balanced on the pedals and strained to hear the sound of any car coming.

He couldn't hear anything coming up the hill. And there were no headlights to be seen.

He leaned well forward to look up and down the road.

The way ahead was clear.

Nate stood up in the saddle, pushed down into the pedals and drew away onto the main road.

*****

Nate was sitting on the kerb in front of a charity shop. He looked at his right foot. He was holding it in his hands. He knew it was his foot. That was his shoe on it. And the shoe was gashed along the outside edge. He wondered how it had happened. His mother would have something to say about that.

And his sock. Blue with white flecks. His mother had bought it. He couldn't remember when. There was ink soaking through it. He couldn't think how it had got ink on it. Not so much ink.

But the ink wasn't ink.

All of a sudden Nate knew that the ink was blood, and it looked like ink because of the light from the orange neon street-lamp near him. His sock was soaked in blood. And it was covering his hands as he held his foot.

His foot seemed very loose. He could wiggle it about from just below the knee.

His knee was stuck out in front of him on the ground, hanging over the gutter, but he couldn't see it because it was covered in torn trouser and dirt.

And the ink that was blood was making a pool in the gutter.

He was very sick.

When he'd finished being sick, Nate's eyes smarted and his head began to pound. Velvet clouds blinded his eyes. Between the bouts of pumping velvet clouds the road went wavy, as if he were looking at it under water.

Then he reeled. Because a pain snatched at him and a fire started where his foot was. It was like no pain he had ever felt before, not even at the worst times running.

Nate made himself go on holding his foot, because he knew he must. He knew it mattered. Nothing else mattered. Only that he wanted to get off the ground.

The velvet clouds and the water in his eyes clashed with the fire in his leg.

And for a while there was nothing.

5. Poor Kid

A worried voice said, "Your name, mate? What's your name?"

The throbbing and the fire and the sickness started again.

And then there was another voice behind Nate – or was it above him? He wasn't sure and couldn't look.

"Poor kid," the second voice said. "He'll have had it if that bloody ambulance doesn't turn up soon."

Faces waving in the water looked at him. Nate realised he was lying down. It was daft to lie down on the ground. So he tried to get up.

He heard a scream. He knew the voice. It was his own. He hadn't wanted to scream like that. But the pain when he tried to get up had made him.

Then there was nothing again.

*****

A two-note siren was wailing.

He didn't like the sound because it beat in his brain.

Now all of him trembled with pain.

Somewhere, lost in it all, was the fire of his leg.

He wasn't holding his foot now or lying on the ground. He wasn't sure what he was doing.

There was just the two-note siren wail, fearful, urgent.

He would be glad if there was nothing again.

And there was.

*****

Nate opened his eyes and a light hurt them. A bright electric light. The fire was still there in his leg, but somehow it was far away. Dulled. His eyes were clearer and the velvet clouds and watery waves had gone. He was lying on a sheet, on a bed.

He saw a woman in a white coat standing on his left. She had grey hair, and deep lines on each side of her mouth.

Nate could see nothing else except the ceiling, which looked patchy. There was a big dirty stain in one corner.

"Still with us then?" the woman said. The voice was not like the voices Nate had heard earlier. This voice was calm and normal. "How do you feel?"

"I'm OK." Nate was surprised at his voice. It was dry and tired. "What's happened?" he asked.

"You were knocked off your bike," the woman said. "But we'll soon have you right. Nothing to worry about."

A nurse appeared on Nate's other side. She was smiling. He felt her take his hand. He could smile back. Before, he hadn't been able to feel anything in his face.

"What's your name?" the woman said.

Somehow it was difficult to remember.

"Nate Clark," Nate said, after a moment.

"Where do you live?" the nurse asked.

He had to struggle even harder for that.

"Longworth Street," he said at last. "Number 56."

"Will your mother or father be in?" she asked.

"I don't know. They should be."

"How old are you?" the woman asked.

"15."

It was an effort to speak. Nate's throat choked and he couldn't swallow.

"Could I have something to drink, please?" he asked.

The nurse pushed his hair from his brow. Her hand felt cool and he realised he was sweating hard.

"Not just yet," she said. "We'll soon have you right."

The woman nodded at the nurse and went out.

The nurse took a swab from a bowl on the table by Nate's bed and started to rub his arm. Nate felt it sore for the first time, and he realised it must be grazed. But it was not a pain that matched the pain of the fire in his leg and he didn't flinch.

The woman's voice came from the corridor. She was talking on the telephone.

"We need to get him into theatre right away," she said. "We may not be able to save the foot. That's right ... The police are contacting the parents ... Good. Be with you soon."

Nate knew the woman was talking about him. Somehow he didn't care. It was all part of the strangeness which had begun on the pavement soon after he left home. That seemed a long time ago.

He kept seeing himself sitting on the kerb holding his foot.

He tried to remember more. To get things straight in his head. To know what had happened. And why. And how.

But he could remember nothing except himself on the pavement holding his foot and thinking about how daft it was to sit there on the ground.

He tried to sit up in the bed now. But his movement brought a rush of twisted, scorching pain which made him call out so that the nurse ran to catch him before he fell back again.

"Lie still, there's a good lad," she said. "Won't be long now."

Nate lay still until they came to wheel him on the bed down a long corridor. Now the nurse was joined by a tall man in a green smock and a green cap that covered all his head. Only his face poking out, a pale patch in the green. He seemed to Nate like something out of a horror film.

The nurse held Nate's hand. They put a mask over his face.

There was nothing again.

6. Fire

For days Nate swayed between life and death.

Now and then he would surface out of the hollow nothingness in which he lay for hours, and feel again the scorching fire in his leg.

One of those times, he saw a thing like a game control on a cable just by his hand. At first he couldn't think what it was for.

Nate tried to think clearly, tried to focus on something other than the fire in him. But his head pounded and he couldn't think for long, and so he gave up.

Then all of a sudden, when his leg not only burned but seemed to twist and tear, and the pain was more than he could bear, his hand grabbed the game control and pushed down on the button. So he came to know what it was for, and it became his best friend, always there when he woke and he would press it.

There were sounds too. Beeps. The ring of a phone. Voices. Sometimes the voices laughed. Sometimes they rose in urgent, fearful calls.

The light around him changed. Sometimes it felt bright and glaring and stung his eyes. Sometimes it was dark and there was a pool of shaded electric light just beyond his bed. This light was a comfort to him, as a beacon comforts sailors. The light, unlike the sounds, was never the same.

None of all this meant much to Nate. It was what he found when he came to. Only the pain meant anything, always there when he woke. He gave his mind to the pain. He began to explore it, to pin-point it in his body.

The worst pain was in his right leg. That was where the fire was – never out, never dull, always the worst of all the pains.

Next was the pain in his head. His head seemed big for a long time, like a balloon. Every sound, every sharp light, every thought hurt his head, lingering like the image on a radar screen. Nate could even feel the uneven pounding of his heart. Feel it. And hear it. Sometimes he saw it as explosions of colour, inside his eyes.

And there were the smaller pains, in his arms and his left side. They never matched the pain in his leg and head. After a while he learned to concentrate on these smaller pains in an effort to distract his tired brain from the big pains. But he could not do it for long.

*****

At last a moment came when Nate drifted out of the nothingness, and felt easier for the first time. His head was clearer. The pains were weaker. After so long it seemed a release. There was pounding and soreness. And the fire still burned, but more dully.

Nate was in a different place now. He turned his head to the left. There were two other beds. A man in pyjamas was sitting propped up in the one nearest. He had an arm in plaster – it was bent so that it looked like a soldier's half way towards a salute. Nate watched to see what the arm would do. It did nothing, just stayed in the silly half-salute. The man was eating biscuits, his knees pulled up, a magazine open on his lap.

Nate thought the arm was funny, and he began to laugh.

Then Nate realised his dad was slumped in a chair on his other side. When he heard Nate laugh, he looked at him like he was seeing a ghost.

"God!" he said. "You scared us, mate! Nurse! Here, nurse! Nate's awake. Come quick!"

Behind his dad, Nate saw another bed, empty this time, then a wall.

He couldn't see straight ahead because his bed rose up in a great hump, neatly covered in sheets and blankets. It looked as if he had an enormous lower half, a sausage instead of legs. That was funny too, and he laughed some more.

7. In Shreds

They took the game control away. It released morphine and Nate didn't need it any more.

Loads of people came to see him. His mum and dad, Jed and Taylor and the captain of the club and some of the team. Some of them had been in when he was in Intensive Care, but Nate hadn't been awake.

"You looked like death, mate." Jed laughed at the thought. "You were all white and your head was swollen and spongy-looking. Right mess you were."

"Didn't I say anything?" Nate was amazed by this picture of him as he'd never seen himself.

"Nothing," Jed said. "You just moaned. Or went a sort of rust-red colour and grabbed that pain-killer button thing and screamed."

"Screamed! Me?" Nate couldn't believe it.

"Worse than a girl. Honest. I scarpered when you screamed like that. Them nurses come running and fussed over you." Jed stopped. He looked round the ward. "Wouldn't mind them fussing over me." He laughed. "Rather be conscious when they did, though."

Nate smiled. "You've got a one-track mind, Jed."

Nate felt better. It was good to be laughing again. The days he couldn't remember were stuck inside him like days in a wilderness. He leaned into the pillows.

When Jed had gone, the doctor Nate had seen the night of the accident came round the ward. Three or four younger doctors in white coats with stethoscopes drooping from their pockets trailed after her. Nurse Walker was beaming at the doctor's side.

"Hello, Nate," the doctor said. "Feeling better?"

"Yes, thanks," Nate said.

“Then I’ve got some good news for you,” she said.

“What’s that?”

“We managed to save your foot. It was like doing a jigsaw. But it’s all there and with a bit of luck we can turn it into a pretty good leg again.”

Nate went cold. It was a shock to realise that his mangled limb was still part of him.

“Don’t worry,” the doctor said. “It’ll take time, but you’ll be as good as new in the end.”

“How long?” Nate’s voice was distant. He was afraid to ask.

“That’s difficult to say. You’ve had a bad accident.” The doctor sat on the edge of the bed. “You remember crossing the junction, do you?”

“Well, I remember starting to cross it,” Nate said. “But after that I don’t remember much more. Not until I came round the other day.”

The doctor looked at the nurse.

“It seems you took off to cross the junction, and there was a car coming up the hill fast. It caught you half way across and the bumper smashed your leg on the frame of your bike. It seems you went over with the bike, and then you crawled away from it and sat on the pavement. It all happened very fast. But the police will want to see you soon. I've kept them away until you could cope."

There was one thing Nate wanted to know. How it all happened didn't matter. In fact, he'd rather not know. He looked at the doctor.

"Doctor, can I ...?" Nate had to force the words. "Will I be able to run again?"

The doctor took a deep breath. "I want to be honest with you, Nate. Your leg's bad, but not so bad we can't make a pretty good job of putting it right again. For normal use, anyway. But the ankle tendon is gone, and I don't think we can do much about it." She stopped a moment, and looked at Nate to check that he understood.

"What does that mean?" Nate asked. His throat was tight.

"It means your ankle will never move normally again."

Nate thought for a moment. “In other words, I won’t ever run well again?”

The doctor shook her head. “I doubt it,” she said.

Nate looked at his hands, folded on the sheet in front of him. They were pale and thin.

“Bit of a mess, isn’t it?” he said.

The doctor stood up. “It is,” she said. “But we’ll look after you like a king here, and before you know it you’ll be running round in a wheelchair like a Formula One driver. And then we’ll get you onto physio.”

The student doctors laughed. Nate looked at them. There were smiles on some faces that were meant to comfort him, professional poker blankness on others. But in all their eyes he saw a look of curiosity. Were they wondering what was going on in his mind now that his body was crippled?

He felt flattened, as though someone had insulted him.

Then they moved away to speak to the man in the next bed.

For the first time since he had come round, Nate forced himself to explore his body below the waist. He knew now that he had been avoiding it.

With his left toes he touched his right leg. He almost jumped at the feel of warm dampness. There was plaster right down the leg, which made it thicker than it should have been, as if the leg had swollen. He slid his right hand down his side and found the rim of the plaster case. But he had found that before. So he returned to the damp plaster just above his ankle.

Nurse Grey, one of the nurses on the ward, was passing.

"Nurse," Nate said. "What is it that's wet near my right foot?"

She glanced at him a moment. "They've told you what happened, have they?"

"Funny, isn't it?" Nate said. "I never thought to check whether it had been chopped off or not. Just thought it had."

"Well, it hasn't," Nurse Grey said. "So you're OK."

"Maybe," Nate said. "But what's the wet?"

"Nothing to worry about. Just a bit of blood seeping through the plaster."

"Seeping through!" Nate was shocked. If blood was still seeping through after all this time, his leg must be in a very bad way. "Still?" he asked.

"Yes," she said. "But it's all right. Don't worry. You're not bleeding to death!"

And with that she strode off.

8. Awake

That was the start of the gloom. First the days of pain. Then the days of depression. Of brooding.

When night came and he slept, Nate would dream the minutes of the crash over and over, and wake sweating and moaning at the horror of it.

Then, one night, the dream changed. He was running. He was in his track gear, and his stride was easy. He was moving without effort, without feeling the ground under his feet. There was no sound of wind or even of his own breath. He saw a car in front of him. It was coming straight at him and he made no effort to avoid it. Just before it hit him, he woke.

Nate lay in his bed in the ward, not sure at first if the dream had been real. He had to go over the real accident in his mind. But there was still an awful gap in his memory after he had started to cross the main road. Nothing till the picture of himself sitting on the pavement.

He heard again the doctor's words. "Soon you'll be running round in a wheelchair."

He stared at the lamp on the nurses' desk, just inside the ward door. The sounds of the others breathing and murmuring in their sleep deepened the loneliness of the night. And the doctor's words closed his mind to other thoughts.

No matter how he tried to find a comfortable way to lie, always below him was the dead weight of the plaster-cased leg.

Nate began to hate his leg. Began to wish they had chopped it off. At least that would have made everything certain. Now it was a chain, like the chain that prevents a prisoner from running. From escaping. From freedom.

"Soon you'll be running round in a wheelchair."

Nate tried to turn onto his side. But the leg stopped him. He sighed.

Nurse Grey padded over to him.

"Not asleep, Nate?" she asked.

He couldn't answer.

"Would you like something to help?" she whispered.

He shook his head. He could smell a trace of scent from her. It was the first time for days he had smelled anything but hospital smells. Somehow it helped.

"Is it bad tonight?" Nurse Grey asked.

"I was dreaming," he said. "Then I woke up and I couldn't sleep again."

He felt the weight of her body and saw the dark shape of her as she sat by his side on the bed.

"How's the leg?" she asked.

She stretched her hand towards him and placed it on his head. It was a soft, cool hand.

"It's all right," he said. "Not too bad. It's the thinking that's worst."

There was silence. Then he felt her hand on his forehead again.

"They've told you I'll never run again?" he said.

"Is that what's keeping you awake?" she asked. "Worrying about running?"

"It's what I loved doing most," he said.

"For now, all you have to do is get well," she told him. "Leave worrying about anything else until later."

"They're going to stick me in a wheelchair," he told her. "I couldn't stand that."

"It's only until your leg can walk again. It'll be better than lying in bed all day."

"It would have been faster if they'd chopped the bloody thing off."

"Faster," she said. "But then you'd be without a leg at all."

"I think I'd have preferred that."

She took her hand from his head.

"You stop chattering and get some sleep," she said. "You're as bad as some of the old men."

Her weight lifted from the bed and she moved away.

But Nate did not sleep for some time.

9. Bits of Paper

One Saturday, at evening visiting time, Jed came with Suj, Steve and Harry. They sat stiff as boards on chairs at either side of his bed. Jed, who had been before, took the lead and teased the nurses to impress the others.

Nate grinned at them. He answered their questions about how he felt with white lies that told them nothing.

"I'm fine," he said. "Much better."

"Team won pretty well today, Nate," Harry said, in his plodding way. "Missed you, of course. Specially for the pace. Slow time, it was."

Suj, always silent, nodded.

Jed growled. "Honest," he said, "they look like snails, they do, Nate. Took thirteen-and-a-half to reach the double stile before the turn back.

Thirteen-and-a-half minutes! We don't just miss you, we need you."

"He's right, Nate," Suj said.

"I tell you," Jed said, "the Harriers aren't going to be the same without you."

"Not ever," Steve said.

"That's what the captain said," Harry muttered.

Ned nodded.

They left a sports magazine behind, spattered with winter rain. There were pictures of footballers with powerful legs, strung with corded muscles, kicking high in the air. They loomed at Nate from every page. Each time he rushed to turn the page. Each time there were more fit bodies caught by the camera. And the Harriers weren't the same without Nate. And they were taking 13.5 minutes to do what he'd done in 10.

Nate stared for one second at the last photo. The last straw. Then he tore the magazine in two. It gave a satisfying rip. He ripped again.

And ripped. And ripped. Cold and deliberate. The pieces fell like autumn leaves about his bed.

The ripping brought Nurse Grey across.

"What's this, then?" she said.

"Bits of paper!" Nate said. He couldn't look at her, but sat defiant.

"Well, tidy it up, please," she said. "I've got more to do than clear up after you."

"Get stuffed!"

The words burst out.

"Excuse me! Don't you dare speak like that to me!" Nurse Grey was fuming, her eyes full of diamonds.

Nate scowled at her. He'd put himself in the wrong and anger at himself tangled with his other feelings.

"I'm sorry," he said. But it was a gruff apology and settled nothing.

Nurse Grey left him surrounded by wounded silence. The other men in the ward cast sharp looks at him and it was a while before talk rang out again.

No one spoke to Nate. Not even the man with the broken arm in the next bed. He sat up with his back half-turned and chatted to the man in the bed next to him. Now and then they'd glance blackly at Nate. He'd committed the worst of sins – he'd been rude to a nurse. You could scream with fear. You could keep the ward awake all night. You could bore people all day long with talk about your operation. All that was expected in hospital. But you couldn't be rude to the nurses. Especially not Nurse Grey – she was the best of the lot.

*****

When his mum and dad came in, Nate could see from their faces that they knew what had happened.

"How are you today, love?" his mum said, with as bright a smile as she could manage.

"You don't look too bad," his dad said.

Nate didn't reply, just watched them both.

His mother sat down and eased off her coat. There were pearls of rain on the puffy fabric. Her nose was red from the cold.

"Nurse Grey says you've been a bit difficult," she said.

"She seemed quite upset, Nate," his dad added.

Nate wished he could say it wasn't like that. His mum looked as if she hoped so too.

"It's the leg and not being able to run again," he mumbled.

There was nothing more he could say. How could he explain everything that made him wish the leg wasn't even there – wish he'd never even ridden a bike at all?

"I know, Nate," his mother said. "But you'll have to stop feeling sorry for yourself if you ever want to get better. There's nothing worse than stress for keeping you ill."

Dad sat in gloom as he listened to them. His elbows were on his knees and his hands clasped in front of him as he watched Nate.

Mum shuffled in her chair. She'd had her say. "It'll not be long till you're out of bed," she said. "As soon as your leg's well enough to make it safe for you to move."

"Mum," Nate said. "Get rid of my bike, will you? I don't want to see it again."

"Not much of it to keep, son," Dad said. "It was all –"

Mum shuddered. "Let's not go into the gory details. Please."

Dad stared at his trainers. Mum's eyes searched the ward again.

"I wish they'd cut the leg off," Nate said.

Dad leaned back in his chair as from a blow.

"You mustn't say things like that, Nathan," his mum said. Her face was shocked and scared. "Doctor Maxwell worked like anything to save it. It took her three hours in theatre, while your dad and me waited. You mustn't wish her good work away."

"No, Nate," Dad said. "She worked an absolute miracle. You'll be thankful, you'll see.

It's just that you still have to come to terms with it. That's the hard part. But you'll do it. Grin and bear it for now."

They left chocolate, soft drinks, grapes and some books when they went. Nate saw them stop and talk to the nurse at the ward door. They looked back at him with worried faces.

"Grin and bear it!"

The words soured in Nate's mind. Just grin and bear the thought that he'd never run again. Grin and bear a limp for the rest of his life, while Jed and the rest of them pounded round the track without him. Grin and bear the people who said how sorry they were, and what a pity it all was. What a pity that such a promising young lad should have such an accident. Yes, what a pity! He'd heard it all before. But this time it was about him.

All right for them, with the two good legs most of them used only to get them in and out of their cars. Wouldn't have made any difference if they'd lost both legs, most of them. And Nate wouldn't have minded if he'd lost his. But he did mind having one mangled, limping leg to drag about. He did mind feeling he had two legs to run with but one of them couldn't. Wouldn't. A leg that was there, but only half-alive, a useless piece of flesh, nagging with pain.

Nate felt disgusted with himself.

The days went by, dragged by, as Nate would have to drag his leg for the rest of his life, slow and painful. The ward became too much to take. It was stuffy and airless. The smell of bodies and disinfectant was awful. The clockwork routines. And the slow, tired march of patients. The dreary, weary, dead life of people who are ill.

His plaster-cased leg trapped him in bed.

Soon, Nate became just another case. He needed no more special care than the others. Then they moved him further down the room, away from the door and the desk and the nurses' constant eye. Then he was among the old men who might have been there since the place was built. It seemed to Nate that they had given up, were just waiting for death.

There were days when Nate lay half-propped up in bed and wished he could die too.

10. A Visitor

Four days later, Jed came in for the evening visit. A packet of chocolate biscuits lay half-finished on Nate's locker top.

"All right, mate," Jed said. "What's with the biscuits? You'll be out of training at this rate."

"So what? I'm out of training for good, anyway."

Jed stood with his hands in his pockets. "Thought you were all for healthy living. It's not like you to stuff your face with rubbish."

"Mind your own business," Nate snapped.

"Touchy tonight," Jed said.

"I'm not touchy at all. Just don't like people interfering."

"Who's interfering? I just said it's not like you to scoff packets of biscuits, that's all."

"All right!" Nate's voice rose sharply. "So it's not like me. It's not like me to be lying around, stuck in bed. But I am. It's not like me to have a mangled leg. But I have. OK?"

"OK," Jed muttered.

But you can't just stand and look at somebody lying in bed. You've got to say something. Jed shifted his feet.

"We're running against Harnsworth on Saturday."

"So?"

Jed shrugged. "Well. Big fixture. Good club, Harnsworth, aren't they?"

Nate reached for another biscuit.

"We beat them last season," Jed said. "Remember?"

"Look, Jed," Nate said. "I couldn't care less if you were running in the bloody Olympics. I don't want to know."

Jed looked bewildered. "What's got into you? First you get at me cos I say something about you eating all them biscuits. Then you go off on one about the Harriers. What am I supposed to do? Sit here and take it?"

"Yes," Nate shouted. "Like I have to take this lying down." He gave his plastered leg a sharp tap.

"Don't blame that on me," Jed said. "I didn't put you there. I'm the one who's come to see you."

"How kind!" Nate's voice cut the air. "I didn't ask you to come. And if all you can do is get at me or witter on about the Harriers, then don't bother to come at all. I'll survive without you."

Jed drew in his breath. He and Nate glared at each other. Then Jed turned away.

"See you!" he spat out and walked down the ward. He didn't look back.

11. New Plaster

Next day, the doctor was round with her shoal of students.

"How's the running champ today?" she said.

"He's a little depressed, doctor," Nurse Walker said. "Not very chatty." She smiled a bleak smile that made Nate feel bad.

The doctor sat on the edge of the bed. "What's the matter, Nate? The leg sore?"

"No, not really," Nate said.

The doctor stood up and moved the blankets at Nate's feet. Nurse Walker stepped in and turned them back for her. She peered at the leg in its white armour. It had a thick, sickly smell. The doctor looked at the raw toes sticking out, and pinched them between her finger and thumb.

"Feel anything?" she asked.

"No."

The doctor looked at the trail of followers.

"The plaster should be changed again, I think," she said.

Nurse Walker replaced the blanket.

The doctor turned back to Nate. "How do you feel otherwise?" she asked.

"Like having my leg chopped off," Nate said. "And sometimes I think I'd rather be dead."

Nate saw the shocked faces of the white shoal. They gave him a flash of pleasure.

The doctor tapped his arm. "Now, now," she said. "That's silly talk, and not at all the right spirit. Work with us and we'll get you in pretty good shape again."

The doctor turned to the nurse as they walked away. "Find a wheelchair for him," she said. "Might cheer him up if he can move about."

The shoal passed on. Nate's curdled feelings remained sour.

*****

The plaster was changed. The new bandage clung to Nate's leg, muddy and itchy.

Nate woke in the middle of the night. The plaster had dried, but his leg itched more than ever. This always happened when the plaster was new. Little bits were rubbed away as his leg moved inside, and the bits made fine powder which irritated his skin. He couldn't scratch.

He lay for an hour, trying to stop the itch by hitting the cast near it. Or he'd push his hand down between the plaster and his leg to reach the spots higher up.

He broke into a sweat. The itching was like torture. And the doctor was the torturer. And this was to go on for months yet. But Nate wouldn't lie there and let them do it.

They could cut his leg off. He didn't care. It would be better. It would be like having a tooth out. Better than letting it hurt for days.

Nate struggled in his half-awake state to pull the leg from the plaster. But it wasn't like taking a foot out of a sock, of course. And so he pushed at the top rim of the case. His leg began to throb.

But he must get his leg out.

The harder he tried, the more he failed, the more determined he became. There was nothing now that mattered in the world but to get his leg out of the plaster.

All of a sudden a piece from the top of the cast broke away and other pieces crumbled round the rim.

That was it – now he just needed something to cut with. Something to split the plaster down the side, just as they had cut his trouser leg away the night he was brought into hospital. They had used a pair of scissors and cut down the seam.

Slowly, silently, so that Nurse Grey wouldn't hear, Nate stretched his hand out until it touched his locker. The locker drawer was open a crack. Nate kept his bits and pieces in there and never bothered to close it. He found the drawer, and he felt about inside. Right at the back, among things which had been in his pockets when he came into hospital, he found his penknife.

He raised his head from the pillows and looked up the ward. Nurse Grey's head shone in the light from her reading lamp she bent over her desk.

Nate opened the knife under the blankets. It wasn't very sharp. He'd used it to clean his running spikes. But at least it had a cutting edge. He had nothing better.

Nate felt the top of the plaster and found the broken patch. He slipped the knife between his leg and the plaster and began work on the split part, sawing up and down. He was surprised how easy it was to cut the plaster away.

By the time Nate reached his knee, he was bent, twisted down the side of the bed, cutting with his right hand and feeling for the path with his left. He felt light-headed and found himself smiling. It was like scrogging apples when he was a kid.

Nate took it easy down his lower leg, scared of what might happen. This was the bad part. He expected any second to feel a terrible bite of pain. Or a warm jet of blood pumping from the uncovered wound. Or sharp bare bone sticking out under the plaster. But nothing happened.

He reached the ankle. This was the hardest part of all. The plaster was thicker there, harder to make any progress at all.

A quarter of an hour later, the plaster was open.

Nate relaxed, lying straight in the bed again.

He scratched his thigh where it was itching. The pleasure was almost painful. He grinned like a cat that had had its ears rubbed. And he felt like purring too.

Sleep came soon afterwards.

12. Up to Something

Nate was still dead to the world when Nurse Grey came round the ward as everyone got their morning tea.

"Come on, Nate. Wakey wakey," she said. "Not like you to be asleep. Must be getting better."

She shook him by the arm. Nate opened his eyes. He wanted to drift off again.

"Go away, nurse," he muttered. He yawned and twisted in bed. A tingling pain blistered in his leg. He jumped.

All of a sudden he remembered what he had done last night. "Oh, hell!" he shouted.

"What's the matter?" Nurse Grey said.

Nate tried to pass it off with a laugh. With his right hand, he searched about under the blankets to make sure that what he remembered was true. It was. Already some of the plaster was like crumbs in the bed.

"Nothing," he said.

"You sure?" Nurse Grey asked. "You looked odd for a minute."

"Yes." Nate stalled. "Well ... it's nothing – just something I remembered." He laughed again.

Nurse Grey studied his face. "You're up to something, Nate," she said.

"No. Honest."

But the nervous laugh came again and that was that. Before he could stop her, Nurse Grey was pulling the blankets back.

She stopped short as her eyes found the crumbs and lumps of sawn-off plaster, and the ruined cast.

She stared for a moment. "So that's it! You ..."

Nate heard no more. For the first time he saw his injured leg exposed. He saw the wreck – the open meat-raw red flesh, and the chunk of bone.

He fainted.

When he came to, Nurse Grey showed not a sign of pity.

"If Sister hears about this, you'll be for it," she said. "It's a good job your foot has stopped bleeding or you'd be in a right mess. Really, Nate!"

The screens went round him. Nurse Grey's shoes squeaked on the polished floor as she sped off. Within minutes she was back again with a young doctor. The young doctor said nothing, but she lifted the blankets, raised her eyebrows, scowled at Nate, dropped the blankets and went away.

Nurse Grey said, "It's a good job for you it was me who found it."

She followed the young doctor out.

Half an hour later, Nate was taken to A&E, where they pushed and pulled him about. The mangled plaster was taken away and a new one put on.

There was none of the kind care he'd always had so far. At times, they hurt him. No one spoke. By the time Nate was back in bed he felt like a child who was in everyone's bad books.

The memory of fainting at the sight of his own leg made him blush.

The new plaster already itched.

The old man in the next bed lay watching him. "In hospital," he said, "you just can't win."

13. Push

Nate sat by the side of his bed with his leg sticking out in front of him. It was white in its new plaster and his toes poked from the end. Even in his dressing-gown with a rug over him, he felt naked. Everyone was staring at him. Nate glowered back.

"You needn't sit there," the nurse said. "We're getting you in a wheelchair."

He felt like a kid in a pram, but it was good to be out of bed.

The nurse gave the chair a push that left Nate stranded between the two rows of beds in the ward.

He sat in the chair, elbows on the arms, and grinned a sarcastic grin. "Grin and bear it," that's what everyone said. Nate would have preferred to throw bricks at the windows. The chair made him feel worse than ever.

There was nothing for it but to push himself out of the way.

He put his hands on the smaller outer rims of the wheels and tried. It took more effort than he had thought. The chair rolled about two metres and stopped. He tried again, and again travelled only a couple of metres.

"Put your back into it!" somebody shouted.

This time Nate thrust with as much force as his arms could manage. The chair shot forward. Slewed. Crashed into a bed. And nearly rammed Nate's plastered foot through his back. He yelled.

The man in the bed he'd rammed smiled. "You have to push with the same weight on each wheel," he said. "Or you'll only turn in circles."

Nate nodded.

He pulled backwards, and found himself facing the way he had come. He had forgotten that to go backwards you have to push hard on the opposite wheel to the way you want to go.

Irritation burned in his stomach. With a determined thrust, he pushed on one wheel and pulled on the other. He was almost surprised to find himself facing in the opposite direction, just as he'd wanted. He had turned almost on the spot.

The next thrusts took Nate smoothly up the ward.

But when he reached the door he was panting from the effort. His arms were already tired and sore.

He looked at the nurse, who had come in to investigate. "Tough work," he said.

She smiled. "It'll get easier as you get used to it. Take it easy now. Not too much at once."

It was ten minutes before Nate had recovered enough to make the return trip.

When Nurse Grey came on duty that evening, Nate had mastered the chair. He had been everywhere in it – the loo, the nurses' office, the café. Places he'd heard about and never seen since he came into hospital. He'd poked his nose here, there and everywhere and learned how to make a sharp turn, or just sweep round. He could rush forward and stop dead – a good way to get on the wrong side of porters and café staff. Backwards, forwards, or round in circles – he could do it all. He had been determined.

Nurse Grey hadn't spoken to Nate since the night of the broken plaster. The sight of him in the chair broke the ice.

"You're up," she said and she didn't hide her smile. "I'm glad."

"Yes. It's OK. I've been going around in this thing all day."

It was almost a surprise to him that he had enjoyed the day. He'd forgotten his leg for hours. He smiled.

Nurse Grey put a hand on each of the chair's arms and leaned towards him. Nate noticed her deep hazel eyes and curly dark hair for the first time.

"You're looking a lot better," she said. "Even your eyes have some sparkle. And your cheeks! Anyone would think you'd been for a run."

He felt the smile drift from his face.

"Sorry," Nurse Grey said. "I've said the wrong thing, haven't I?"

Nate shrugged. "Don't worry. Maybe I can go for a run in this thing soon."

They both chuckled, glad of a joke to ease the moment.

"I'll tell you what," Nurse Grey said. "As soon as you've got used to it, I'll take you out one afternoon before I come on duty. How about it?"

"It's a deal," Nate said.

14. News

Nate's mum wanted to make out the wheelchair was the best thing ever.

"Up and about!" she said. "That's great, isn't it, Neil?"

Nate's dad sat on the visitor's chair, mouth in a tight smile.

Nate's mum didn't wait for his dad to answer. "The nurse said when we came in that she's never seen such a change. You must be feeling much better in yourself, Nate. Are you?"

"I'm OK. The chair took some getting used to, but I've done it."

"The nurse said you managed the chair as well as anyone she's seen," his dad said.

"It's not that hard, Dad."

His dad nodded. His mum leaned towards him.

"They say they're going to move you soon." She talked in a loud whisper that even the deaf old man in the next bed could hear.

"Are they? When?"

"Don't know. A day or two. Depends how you get on."

She paused. Nate knew it was one of those times when he had to ask all the questions. It was Mum's way of being dramatic.

"Where are they putting me, then?" he asked.

His mum looked round to see if anyone was listening. "I think," she said, "they're putting you in neurosurgery."

"Neurosurgery?" Nate asked. "What have nerves got to do with my leg?"

"Nothing," Mum said. "But they do skin grafts there too."

"Oh," Nate said. "Well, that's something to look forward to."

15. Jamie

When the visitors had gone, Nurse Grey came down the ward to Nate's bed. He was still sitting in the chair. He felt tired. The work with the chair during the day and his mum's chatter had worn him down. He was brooding on the way a bashed-up leg knocked the energy out of you. And brooding about having new bits stuck on.

Nurse Grey stood in front of him. She looked cool and neat.

"Can you cope with a trip along the main corridor?" she asked. It was clear she could see the tiredness in his face. "Or would you prefer to wait until tomorrow?"

"Has everyone gone?" Nate said. He tried to smile.

"All the vistors, yes."

"That's OK then," he said. "I don't need everyone watching me. Come on, let's go."

Nurse Grey pushed Nate towards the door. "Feeling self-conscious?" she asked. "Everyone does at first. You'll soon get used to it."

She backed out the doors, which swung closed after them, and wheeled Nate into a long flat corridor that was like the stalk in a leaf, with the wards branching off on each side. It was wide and tiled with rubber so that there was little noise from people's shoes. It smelled of polish and disinfectant and the medical smells that always hung in the air. It was colder there too.

"All right. Now let me see you push yourself to the end and back," Nurse Grey said. "If you can do that, you're safe to go anywhere in the hospital."

"My road test, eh?" Nate smiled.

"That's it."

Nate didn't like showing off. This was his first time out of the ward with someone else since he came in – well, when he was awake anyway. He felt that in some way he was on trial. At least the corridor was empty.

"Here we go then," he said, but there was no life in his voice.

Nate went off down the corridor. Once he got the chair moving, it ran easily. As he passed one of the spaces between two wards he saw a boy sitting on a bench. Nate looked away and pushed the chair faster.

At the end, he turned and began the return trip. Far along the corridor he could see Nurse Grey. She waved.

It was a real effort to push now. Nate's leg began to throb.

Then he saw the boy. He stood up and watched Nate pushing towards him. He had a small camera in his hands. As Nate approached, the boy raised it to his face.

The light flashed. He'd taken a picture of Nate in the wheelchair.

Nate thrust forward hard and swept up to the boy. The boy was grinning all over his face.

Nate snatched the camera out of the boy's hands. The boy's grin turned into open-mouthed surprise.

"Hey! What are you ..."

Nate tore the back off the camera. "Shut up!" he shouted.

Nurse Grey had started walking towards them. Now she broke into a run. Her feet echoed.

"Nate!" she cried.

Nate was pulling the film from the inside of the camera. Like a dead animal's guts.

"Those are my pictures!" the boy cried. "You're wrecking them!"

Nate forced the boy away with his elbow.

The film came out, torn. Nate crumpled it and threw it behind him. The boy grabbed his camera back.

Nurse Grey arrived, breathing hard. "Nate, stop!" she yelled. "What are you doing?"

"He took a picture, the little sod."

“What’s the matter, Nate?” Nurse Grey asked. “It was only a photo.”

“He shouldn’t take pictures like that,” Nate snapped.

“I didn’t mean to upset you,” the boy said.

“Just cos I’m stuck in a bloody wheelchair,” Nate grumbled.

“Don’t you swear at Jamie,” Nurse Grey said. “He didn’t mean any harm.”

“To hell with Jamie. He can stuff his camera.”

Nate trundled off up the corridor as fast as he could go.

Behind him, he heard Nurse Grey. “It’s all right, Jamie,” she said. “I’ll see you get another film.”

“Don’t worry, nurse. It’s OK. It doesn’t matter.”

‘Doesn’t matter! It does matter,’ Nate thought. If you were the one in the wheelchair, it mattered. His shoulders hurt.

Nurse Grey's squeaky shoes came up behind him. She forced the chair into the nurses' office in the corridor that led off their ward.

Then she stood in front of Nate, her arms folded, her eyes sparking.

Nate sat still and dumb.

"I suppose you're very pleased with yourself," Nurse Grey said. "Now that you've vented your bad temper on someone again."

Nate breathed hard. "That kid should know better than to take photos without asking."

Nurse Grey's tone was acid. "Maybe. But that's no reason for you to behave like you did."

"Look! I've told you," Nate almost yelled. "I don't like being seen in this stupid chair. I don't like it. I feel like a car crash with everyone staring. You don't expect people to take your photo when you're rolling round hospital corridors like a wreck."

Nurse Grey turned away.

"All right! I understand," she said. "But you're still behaving like a child. You ruined his film."

"It's his own fault," Nate said. "It'll teach the little loser. It's all the same with people like him. They've got no idea what it's like to be me. Sick, in a wheelchair. It's just one big joke to them."

There was a minor earthquake. Nurse Grey's white uniform blurred. The room vibrated with a furious "WHAT!"

It took Nate's breath away. And there was Nurse Grey's face right up close to his, her anger hot enough to be felt.

"Do you know who that 'little loser' is?" she asked, her voice ice cold. "Do you know who the boy that doesn't know about sick people is? Do you?"

She waited. Nate sensed his execution was near.

"No," he muttered. "Who?"

"That's Jamie Thorpe."

"So? Who's Jamie Thorpe when he's at home?"

"You don't know about Jamie Thorpe?" Her voice was cutting. "Then let me tell you. Jamie's not a kid. He's 15."

"So why so small?" Nate asked.

"I shouldn't tell you this. It could get me in trouble. But I'm going to. Jamie hasn't grown as he should because he has a serious heart defect."

Nate felt himself go numb.

Nurse Grey went on. "If he does anything too energetic his heart could give up and he'd die. He might die soon anyway. He's already had loads of operations to put it right. Now he has to have another. And this time there's more chance he'll die than survive. But despite all that, he's spent half his life fund-raising for this hospital. He's been in the paper about once a month since he was born."

She paused for a moment. "That's your stupid loser who doesn't know anything about being ill."

Nurse Grey eased away from Nate. He was glad. He felt sick and weak.

"He's the boy you swore at and whose film you tore up," she said, with no acid or coldness in her tone now.

She didn't need to push the point. Nate was thinking it already. The sick feeling got worse. It was disgust at himself. The weakness made his hands shake, from horror at what he had done. His throat went tight and his eyes swam, so that he felt he would cry. He took a deep breath. And tightened his lips.

Nurse Grey had walked behind him. Maybe she had seen what he felt. She stood behind him, while Nate felt things but couldn't think, knew things but couldn't work them out. The last months passed through his mind as pictures here and there, out of order and scattered in forgotten days in bed.

At last Nate spoke. "I've been a total loser myself, haven't I?"

Nurse Grey drew up a chair and sat by his side. Nate stared ahead. And at his hands. And then he snatched a look at her.

"Not just with Jamie either, you know," she said. "The way you've sulked and let yourself get moody hasn't helped anybody much."

Nate nodded. "I know," he said.

He looked at Nurse Grey and saw that the anger had left her. She sat still beside him.

"Would you do something for me, nurse?" Nate asked.

"Yes. Of course."

"Before you come in tomorrow, will you buy me some new rolls of film?"

She laughed at him, but it was a kind laugh. "I'd love to," she said. "I'll have to order them online, so it'll take a day or two."

"Thanks."

"Don't mention it," she said.

"Sorry I've been so crappy," he said.

"Over now. Let's forget it."

16. Ward 18

Three days later Nate sat in his wheelchair all day. He had put on a long-sleeved T-shirt and a hoodie, which was warmer than his pyjamas and made him feel fitter – part of the everyday healthy world.

For a long time he sat and watched every movement outside the ward door. Now and then he pushed himself into the main corridor so that he could see all the way up and down. All the time he was waiting for Nurse Grey. He knew she wouldn't come until late in the afternoon. He couldn't help himself. He couldn't settle to read or talk to the others. He waited like a man who has something important to do, which squeezes all else from his mind.

She came into the ward sooner than he expected but long after the waiting had made him grumpy. At first he didn't recognise her. She was in normal clothes. Nate had never seen Nurse Grey in anything but a nurse's uniform. Now she was in jeans and boots and a green top.

"Hi," she said.

She dropped a parcel onto his knee. "There's the film you wanted. I checked the kind he uses."

"Thanks." Nate looked at her, not sure of himself. "I thought I'd take it down to Jamie myself."

She nodded, pleased. "That's a good idea," she said. "I'd go now, if I were you. He's in Ward 18. I saw him as I came up. I'll see you when you get back to hear how things have gone."

"Thanks, nurse."

"Serena," she said.

"Thanks, Serena."

17. Let's Go

Nate pushed his way to Ward 18.

A nurse was standing in the corridor with a tray of little bottles in her hands.

"Hi there," she called. "You must be Nate Clark."

"Yes. How do you know?"

"Nurse Grey said you'd be in."

"And did she say I'd be wanting Jamie Thorpe?"

"She did. He's in the ward sitting by his bed."

"Could I talk to Jamie somewhere else?" Nate asked.

"There's a visitors' room. Talk to him there. I'll tell him you want him."

Nate bowled himself into the room. There were worn chairs and a big bowl of tired flowers on a table. He placed himself opposite the door, so that he was facing it.

In a moment Jamie came in. He seemed even smaller now Nate knew his real age. Nate kept thinking of the weak heart inside him. Jamie's camera hung over his shoulder.

"Hi, Nate." Jamie walked over to Nate. "Sorry I made you so cross the other day. If I'd known you were feeling that touchy I wouldn't have done it."

Words spurted out of Jamie. As though he had a lot of talking to do in a short time.

"No," Nate said. "It was my fault. You know – I mean your camera."

"That's nothing." Jamie smiled. "I want to be a photographer, you see, so I need to learn how to take all kinds of shots."

"Sounds good," Nate said. "I've brought you this. Since I spoiled the other one."

He handed the parcel to Jamie.

"That's great of you. Thanks. But you shouldn't have bothered. I've got plenty."

"Yes, but I shouldn't have torn the other one out. So this is to replace it."

Jamie was pleased. "I'll tell you what," he said. "I could take you to the far end of the hospital. We could take some photos."

Nate didn't know. He thought of the heart with a fault and Jamie pushing the wheelchair.

"If you're worried about my heart, forget it," Jamie said. "I'll be OK. I've done all sorts of things that are supposed to wreck me and I'm still here. Anyway, you can push yourself most of the way. How about it?"

They could see from the window that it was a fine sunny afternoon. The beginning of spring. Nate wanted to be outside. To feel fresh air again. To hell with it! What did the chair matter? And Jamie said he could manage most of it himself.

"Let's go, then," Nate said.

Jamie opened the door and peeped round into the corridor. He looked back and winked.

They got into the corridor. They could see a nurse on the other side of the window in the ward doors. She was flitting from bed to bed with her tray.

"All clear," Jamie said.

They sneaked out into the main corridor like two kids skiving school. Then Nate pushed himself.

Jamie walked along beside the chair. It was slow going. Before Nate's ward, Jamie ran ahead. He looked down the ward corridor, then turned and waved. Nate pushed on until they were on the other side, out of sight of the nurse in his own ward.

All the hospital staff who passed them spoke to Jamie. Everyone was used to seeing him about.

They were almost at the outside door when they heard Nurse Grey calling from behind them. "Nate. Jamie."

They stopped in their tracks. Like criminals discovered.

"And what's all this?" She was smiling the way a teacher smiles at naughty kids she likes.

"Well, you see," Jamie said, "we thought we'd just have a little bit of exercise."

"If the doctor catches you ..."

"If the doctor catches us," Jamie butted in, "we'll blame it all on you. Say you told us to go. OK?"

Jamie looked at Nate. Nate looked at Jamie. They both looked at Nurse Grey and nodded. Together.

Nurse Grey laughed. "In that case, I'd better come along too – just to see you're comfortable and taken care of, you understand."

Jamie pulled a monster scowl.

Nate drew in his breath loudly.

"Nurses can be such a pain, can't they?" Jamie said.

"Some more than others, of course," Nate said.

Jamie's eyebrows went up. "Oh, yes! Some much more than others."

Nurse Grey waited with simmering patience, watching their double act.

"What do you think?" Jamie said. "Is this one OK?"

Nate considered. "OK, yes, she'll do," he said.

Jamie turned to Nurse Grey. "You have our permission to accompany us, Nurse Grey," he said. And bowed.

They all laughed.

"Before we go, warm clothes for you," Nurse Grey told Nate. "And I'm Serena to you two this afternoon."

She was gone before he could object. She brought back a jacket and made him put it on.

18. Action Shots

They went off into the road, out of the hospital grounds. Out to the streets of the smart end of town where the hospital was. Out to a path that led across a little park and along a path by a river. Small. Not very deep. But clear.

The trees were still bones but with buds on. And the path was muddy so that in parts it was a struggle for Serena to push the wheelchair. But the sun shone and the water glinted. And Jamie kept up a constant patter, sprinkled with jokes that were almost too cheesy to laugh at.

"Did you hear what happened when I had my operation?" he was saying when they stopped to rest on a bench by the stream. Serena and Jamie sat there. Nate in his chair, his white plaster-covered leg stuck like a club in front of him. Serena, her sides sore with laughter and tears rolling down her face. Jamie, bobbing, words tumbling out, his face red from talking so much.

A man with a dog tried to pass them. The dog took fright at Serena's cascade of giggles and flew off down the track the way they had come. The man followed, whistling and shouting. Shouting the dog's name – Buster. That made them laugh even more.

By the time they had simmered down, Buster was back on his lead. Man and dog went by – the man disgusted and angry as well as out of puff, Buster shivering and glaring from angry eyes as he passed.

"I'm going to take some photos," Jamie said. He got up, prepared his camera and sized up Serena and Nate.

"Don't take us," Nate said.

"Sure, why not?" Jamie said. "Smile, please. Say cheese."

Serena and Nate made snapshot faces. Wide, unnatural grins and eyes squinting in the sun.

But Jamie wasn't finished. He wandered round like a hunter stalking. Before they knew what was happening, he had taken three from odd, interesting angles.

"Enough of you celebs," he said at last. "I'm off to find something more exciting. Be back soon."

Serena and Nate looked at the water and the fields on the other side. It seemed very quiet after their laughter and the man shouting and Buster barking and Jamie prattling on.

"You'd never think he's having a serious operation in a couple of days' time," Serena said.

"What? Jamie? His big op? In two days?"

Serena nodded. Nate was shocked.

"Does he know?" he asked.

"Yes."

"What are his chances?"

Serena threw a pebble into the stream. Rings exploded over the surface.

"If he doesn't have it, he'll not live much longer. If he does, there's about a 50–50 chance he'll come out of it."

Nate watched the rings pulsate into the bank. And die.

"Poor kid," he said.

Serena tucked her feet under her and sat facing Nate in his chair.

She sighed. "Jamie will be all right, I think. He's got Rasool for the operation. He's a brilliant surgeon."

They sat, quiet. Nate watched the stream.

"Don't you get fed up with ill people?" he said.

Serena bent down and pulled a spiny blade of grass. "I get fed up. But just with the long hours and being on the go all the time. I don't get fed up with the people. You can't really get fed up with people when they're depending on you."

"But some of the old boys in the ward take advantage," Nate said. "Look at the way they have you running around for them. Lazy old sods."

Serena laughed at his anger for her.

"They're no bother," she said. "Not like you!" She grinned at him and put out her tongue.

Nate grinned back, then stuck out his tongue too.

"Got you!" Jamie stood square in front of them with his camera.

Nate flung himself back in his chair. "You didn't ...!"

Jamie rubbed his hands in glee. "Blackmail," he growled. "I also have here," he said, searching his pockets, "three choc ices which I snapped up at bargain winter prices from a shop along the way."

Serena pulled a face. "Choc ices in winter. You're mental, Jamie!"

The ices were squashy and squashed, cold and messy. Nate thought they tasted all the sweeter for being eaten outdoors on this cold day.

"We'd better go," Serena said, pulling tissues from her pockets so they could wipe their hands. She pushed Nate back onto the path.

It was near dusk and already colder. They walked back a bit faster. Jamie was less chatty. The high-jinks seemed to have evaporated. It was enough for the three of them to be together.

At the hospital gate, as they turned in, the sun broke from some low cloud near the horizon, very red. Trees were tinted, and houses set on fire. Long shadows patchworked the ground.

"That's a super light," Jamie said. "Let's take another photo. No mucking about this time." He laughed as he set the camera. It was a neat, expensive one.

Nate had a sudden thought.

"No," he said. "Give it to me. We'll have one of you. Bet you never have one taken. Always making other people suffer."

"No," Jamie said, and he stepped back out of grabbing range of Nate's chair. "Don't be daft."

But Serena put her arm round him. "Yes," she said. "One of you. Come on. Give Nate the camera."

Jamie was beaten. "All right, then. Where do you want me?"

He ran to a lamp-post, swung round it at arm's length and stopped in mid-swing. "How about this?" he said.

"You look like one of my mum's sad old 80s pop posters." Nate raised the camera to his eye. "Done," he said. "And for some reason the camera is still OK."

'And the day after tomorrow,' he thought, 'Jamie is going to be lying in an operating theatre having his heart cut into.' But Jamie didn't seem to be worried about it. It might just have been a trip to the dentist.

Outside Nate's ward they stopped.

"I'll see you tomorrow," Nate said.

"Can't," Jamie said. "They'll make me stay in bed all day. Ready for my op the next day."

Nate looked at Serena. She was behind him, her hands on the chair.

"Will they?" he asked.

She nodded.

"Well then," Nate said. He felt weak all of a sudden, tight in the chest.

Jamie stood in front of him, hands stuck in his trouser pockets and his camera slung across his body.

"Well then," Nate said again. "I'll see you after the op."

"Yes. Fine. OK." Jamie looked hard at him a moment.

He seemed calm now, the bounce and the words all gone, a lone boy in a corridor looking at a nurse and a young man in a wheelchair. Then his smile spread over his face again.

"See he doesn't run away, nurse," he said.

Serena smiled back. "I will, Jamie. Best of luck with the op."

"That's nothing," Jamie said. "Catch you later."

He walked off.

Serena and Nate watched him go down the corridor. He didn't turn to look back. But he waved a hand in the air before he disappeared into his own ward.

19. Waiting

The day of Jamie's operation crawled. Minutes ground by. The day seemed quieter than usual. As if there was less movement. Fewer comings and goings. Not as much rustle and bustle.

Jamie was taken to the theatre at nine in the morning.

Nate wheeled himself into the main corridor, but the bed with Jamie in it went the other way to the theatre and didn't pass him.

Every time Nurse Walker passed, Nate asked if Jamie was out yet. She shook her head and said nothing.

It was afternoon before word came that the operation was over and Jamie was in recovery.

"He's all right," Nurse Walker said. "That part went well anyway."

The weight of the morning lifted.

"That's fine then," Nate said.

"Fine so far," Nurse Walker said. "But he's not out of the woods yet. He has to get through the next day or so before the danger is over. You can't tinker with somebody's heart and expect them to laugh it off, you know."

"If anybody can take it laughing, Jamie can," Nate said.

"True," the nurse said. "You're a bit hot. You all right?"

"Fit as a fiddle. Just nerves, for Jamie."

Nurse Walker gave him a look, then went to the next bed.

20. A Small Box

The afternoon was filled with the snores of the men in the ward, their sleepy coughs and splutters. The ones who were awake watched TV with their headphones on. They got up, if they could, and sat about talking and drinking tea. Nate could hear now and again the laughs of the nurses.

A doctor wandered in and out again. Then a young man was wheeled in after an appendix operation. He looked white and thin and helpless.

Nate thought of Jamie, lying just like that too. Struggling under it all to keep his body alive. This man would get well. But Jamie had to fight to live. It was happening everywhere in the hospital. People fighting to keep life in them, because in the end that was what mattered.

Nate had never thought of it while he panted round the training runs all those weeks ago. Why should he? But it had been there all the time. A few miles away, but like a different world.

Nurse Grey appeared in the ward an hour before she was due on duty. She was with another nurse that Nate recognised.

"Can I have a word, Nate?" Serena asked. She pulled the curtain around his bed.

The other nurse was from Jamie's ward. She had a small red and green box in her hands. She looked strained and drawn. Her eyes were wet.

She handed Nate the box.

"What's this?" he asked.

The nurse opened her mouth, but no sound came.

"Before they took Jamie to the theatre he gave that box to Nurse Wilson," she said. "He said that if he didn't make it you were to have it."

Nate swallowed. "You mean Jamie's dead?"

It sounded a hollow thing to say. A strange, new and difficult word.

Serena gave a slight nod. “An hour ago,” she said.

Nate looked at the box. At the bright red and green paint. His name was scribbled over the top in big-lettered writing.

Without looking up, he said, “Thanks for this, nurse.”

There was a silence. Then the nurse left.

There was nothing to say. None of the questions Nate wanted to ask seemed important. Neither he nor Serena moved for a while.

Then, at last, he opened the box. Carefully, without tearing it. The box was a worn, old cardboard one. Inside, there was some tissue paper. In the paper was Jamie’s camera. Nate took it out.

He remembered snapping Jamie as he hung from the lamp-post.

He looked at Serena. She smiled through tears.

There was an envelope too. Nate took out a note and some photographs.

The first picture was of Nate and Serena – the photo Jamie had taken on the river bank when they didn't know he was there. Nate smiled at the picture of him poking his tongue out. There were the others too, the ones taken from odd angles, and the one of Serena and Nate making "say cheese" faces at the camera.

Under them all was Nate's photo of Jamie hanging round the lamp-post. Nate could almost hear his laughter.

He passed the photos to Serena and read the note.

It was written in the same big letters.

If you get this I won't need it any more. And I'd like you to have it.

Hope your leg is well soon.

See you at the big party in the sky.

Jamie

Nate passed the note to Serena. She read it. And passed it back. Nate read it again. The big, open, swift letters seemed as much like Jamie as the photo of him.

"Makes it sound as though what's happened today doesn't matter," Nate said, at last.

"Maybe it doesn't."

Nate blew his nose. "Maybe you learn more in a couple of days than you've ever learned before."

Serena gave him a hug. "I know what you mean," she said. "Now I must go on duty. And then we have to get you ready for your first skin graft tomorrow."

Nate thought it was odd that now he should feel almost like he used to after a long run, and a shower, when back at home. Changed in himself, with a better connection to the world.

Ready to do his best. Ready for whatever might come next.

Our books are tested
for children and young people by
children and young people.

Thanks to everyone who consulted on
a manuscript for their time and effort in
helping us to make our books better
for our readers.

More from **Barrington Stoke ...**

The Devil's Angel

KEVIN BROOKS

There was no fuss. Dean just walked into the classroom. Sat down. Smiled. Then beat another kid to a pulp.

It's half way into the summer term of Year 10 when Dean storms into Jack's life. Dean's scary, but he's exciting too, and soon the two boys are on course for a summer that will change their lives for ever.

Brock

ANTHONY McGOWAN

Life's not easy for Nicky. His mum's gone, his dad's on bail, and his brother Kenny needs looking after like a kid.

When Kenny drags Nicky out of bed one dark morning, Nicky has no idea that he is about to witness a terrible act of destruction, and the senseless killing of an innocent animal. But Nicky manages to save something precious from the disaster, and his and Kenny's lives are changed for ever.

Moose Baby

MEG ROSOFF

They were all waiting to say 'I told you so'. Jess's mum. The midwives. Her boyfriend's mum and dad. 'I told you you should be careful.' 'I told you you wouldn't cope.' 'I told you that girl was bad news.' Jess was ready for it all. Bring it on. She just wasn't ready for a moose baby. Whatever Jess thought she was expecting, she wasn't expecting this.

Over the Line

TOM PALMER

It's the proudest moment of Jack's life – his debut as a professional footballer. But it's 1914 and the world is at war. Talk of sportsmen's cowardice leads to the formation of a Footballers' Battalion and Jack has little choice but to join up. Jack and his team-mates will have to survive a waking nightmare if they are ever to play football again.

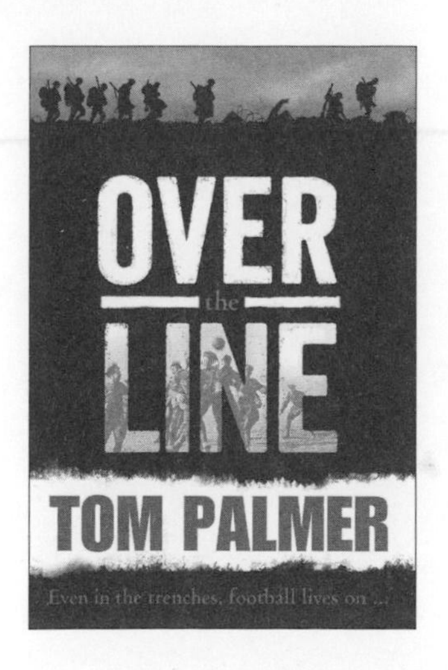

www.barringtonstoke.co.uk